Born in Blindness of Pride, Only to Awaken in the Fear of The Living God

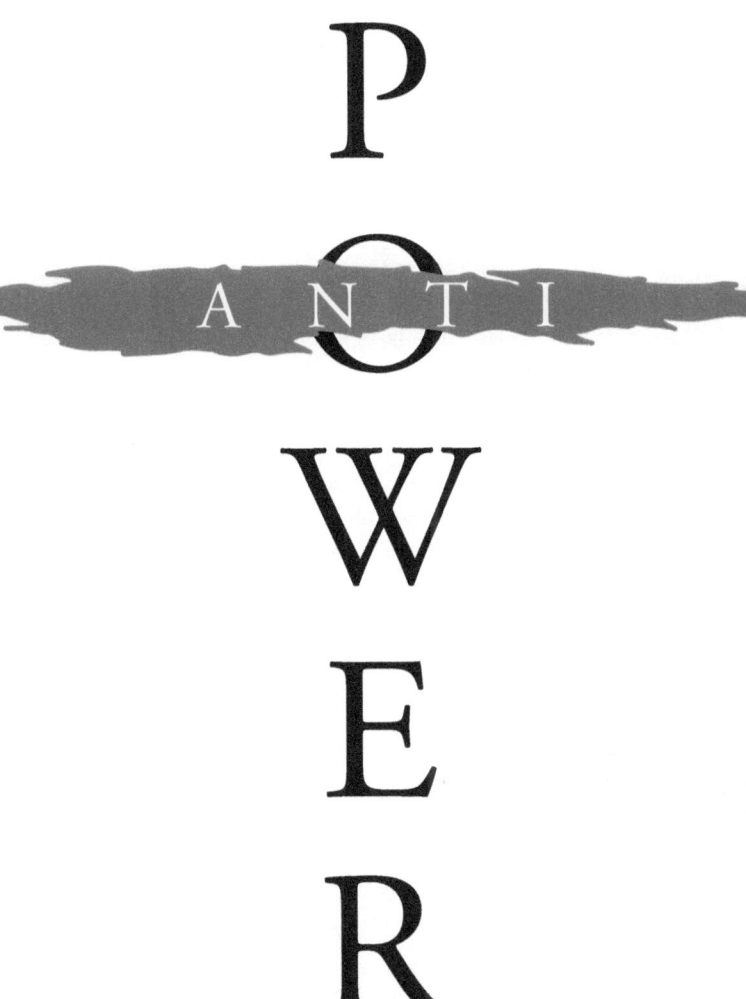

P
ANTI O
W
E
R

Written by the Sinful Soldier and Beautiful Queen

MEGO ISKANDAR
ROSA AGUILAR

MILTON & HUGO L.L.C.
4407 Park Ave., Suite 5
Union City, NJ 07087, USA

Website: *www. miltonandhugo.com*
Hotline: *1- 888-778-0033*
Email: *info@miltonandhugo.com*

Ordering Information:
Quantity sales. Special discounts are granted to corporations, associations, and other organizations. For more information on these discounts, please reach out to the publisher using the contact information provided above.

Library of Congress Control Number: 2025902534
ISBN-13:   979-8-89285-469-6   [Paperback Edition]
                  979-8-89285-468-9   [Digital Edition]

Rev. date: 01/22/2025

Chapter

1

Innocence and Desire

In the beginning there was a baby boy. Born into a world of purity and promise, he entered *Creation* by the *Hand* of *The Creator.* His heart was light, untouched by the burdens of the world. He had dreams, though simple, of success and fulfillment. Yet his desires were untainted, for he knew nothing of the complexities and possessions that would later cloud his soul.

And said, "Assuredly I say to you, unless you are converted and become as little children, you will by no means enter the kingdom of heaven."

—*Matthew 18:3 (NKJV)*

This verse emphasizes the purity, innocence, and untainted spirit of a child, resonating with the theme of the boy's beginnings in a world of simplicity and promise. It also sets a spiritual tone that aligns with the overarching theme of innocence and divine creation.

Chapter

2

The Journey into the Unknown

Years passed, and the boy, now growing into a young man, began to experience the purity of life. The world, at first so welcoming, began to show him its complexities. He reveled in the beauty of it all, believing the world to be good, but something darker started to stir inside him. He grew heavier, not just in body but in soul. The innocence of his youth was slowly overtaken by the weight of regret and emotional turmoil. He tried to fill the emptiness with indulgence and merriment, but soon the boy found himself lost in gluttony and self-loathing.

The world around him began to mock him. His body, once a symbol of life and purity, was now ridiculed for its imperfections. He was called abnormal, cursed, and unlovable. In his isolation, the boy felt the sting of rejection and the growing darkness inside him. The pure soul he once was, had been shattered.

The Lord is near to those who have a broken heart, And saves such as have a contrite spirit.

—Psalm 34:18 (NKJV)

This verse reflects the young man's emotional turmoil, his feelings of rejection, and the growing darkness within. It also offers a glimmer of hope, showing that even in the depths of his despair, God remains near and offers redemption and healing. It ties the narrative of struggle to the potential for divine grace and salvation.

Chapter

3

The Fall into Darkness

As the boy continued his journey, he began to question the purpose of his existence. Life felt like a never-ending routine. He had once dreamed of success, but now, he merely survived. The weight of others' expectations crushed him, and a voice began to whisper within him, urging him to seek validation at any cost. The boy, desperate for approval, began to adopt the behaviors and beliefs of those around him, not understanding that in doing so, he was losing himself.

The boy fell into sin, thinking that if everyone else did it, it must be acceptable. He picked up bad habits, believing they would numb the pain and time itself. Yet no matter how much he indulged in evil, it never satisfied. It was as if his soul was slipping further into the abyss, leaving him empty and broken.

For the wages of sin is death, but the gift of

God is eternal life in Christ Jesus our Lord.

—Romans 6:23 (NKJV)

This verse captures the essence of the body's fall into sin and the emptiness it brings. It reflects the spiritual death and separation from God caused by his choices while also subtly pointing toward the hope of redemption and eternal life through grace, setting the stage for potential transformation.

Chapter

4

The Search for Redemption

In the depths of his despair, the boy's heart ached for meaning. He was trapped in a cycle of sin and self-doubt, unable to escape the pain. Yet something inside him refused to give up. He longed for peace, for something greater than himself to pull him from the darkness.

It was then that he met the beautiful Queen. She was everything he had longed for—pure, radiant, and untainted by the world's cruelties. For a moment, the boy felt hope. He believed she could be his salvation, a beacon of light in his otherwise bleak existence. But even in the presence of this beautiful Queen, the boy found no peace. His past sins, his father's rejection, and his own brokenness gnawed at him.

Come to Me, all you who labor and are heavy laden, and I will give you rest. Take My yoke upon you and learn from Me, for I am gentle and lowly in heart, and you will find rest for your souls.

—Matthew 11:28–29 (NKJV)

This verse beautifully reflects the boy's longing for redemption and peace. It emphasizes that true rest and healing come not from earthly sources, like the Queen, but from surrendering to God. It aligns with the boy's internal struggle and his yearning for a greater force to rescue him from his pain.

Chapter

5

A Moment of Clarity

The boy's life seemed to be spiraling out of control. His sins multiplied, and he felt disconnected from the world and from himself. He turned to destructive behaviors, trying to numb the pain that never seemed to go away. The Queen, once a symbol of hope, now seemed to drift away as the boy's darkness deepened.

One night, in a moment of reckoning, the boy's insides were aflame. He went to the mirror and gazed into his own eyes; the boy saw something he could not deny. His soul understood he saw not himself but a twisted reflection—an evil creature formed from the years of anger, pride, and rejection. It was a moment of clarity, a realization that he had become something he never intended. His soul, once pure, was now tainted.

The boy then ran away and felt like an empty vessel. But in that moment of despair, something shifted. *A mighty hand*, unseen yet undeniable, touched the boy's mind and wiped *his mighty hand* across his mind. The boy understood it was *the Creator*, guiding him back from the brink of destruction. The boy felt a wave of emotions—fear, love, sorrow, and hope—all at once! And at that moment, he knew the *truth*: he had been given a second chance.

Therefore, if anyone is in Christ, he is a new creation; old things have passed away; behold, all things have become new.

—*II Corinthians 5:17 (NKJV)*

This verse perfectly encapsulates the boy's moment of clarity and the transformative power of God's intervention. It reflects the shift from despair to hope, the realization of his brokenness, and the promise of a new beginning through divine grace and redemption. It highlights the boy's second chance and *The Creator's* hand guiding him back to the path of righteousness.

Chapter

6

The Battle Within

The boy, now a man, struggled with his past. The weight of his sins was heavy, and yet he could not escape *the Savior's* grace. The battle raged within him—between the man he had become and the boy he once was. He sought redemption—not just for himself, but for the Queen he has failed. He wanted to change, restore his soul, and align his desires with the will of *the Savior.*

As he sought peace, the boy found himself facing his father again. He had tried for years to gain his father's approval, but it was never enough. Now, with the wisdom he had gained through his struggles, the boy realized that his father's rejection had been a part of the journey. It had shaped him, but it no longer defined him.

For I delight in the law of God according to the inward man. But I see another law in my members, warring against the law of my mind, and bringing me into captivity to the law of sin which is in my members.

—Romans 7:22–23 (NKJV)

This verse reflects the internal struggle the man faces between his past sins and his desire for redemption. It highlights the spiritual battle within, aligning with the theme of wrestling with one's old self while seeking a path toward *the Savior*.

Chapter

7

Embracing *the Savior*

The boy's transformation was not instantaneous, but it was real. *The Savior* showed him that *He* banged on his door multiple times instead of knocking and kept missing the opportunity for salvation. He immediately turned to *the Savior* for guidance, seeking *wisdom* and understanding. His life was no longer about success in the world's eyes but about living in accordance with a higher purpose. He felt the presence of *the Savior* in everything—the animals, the beauty of *Creation*, and even the struggles he faced.

The boy, now a man full of *wisdom* and virtue, began to understand the true nature of *peace*. It was not found in success or validation but in alignment with the *Creator's* will. The battle against sin was not over, but the man now had the strength to fight it. He was no longer a victim of his past but a soldier for good, standing firm in his newfound faith.

Behold, I stand at the door and knock. If anyone hears My voice and opens the door, I will come in to him and dine with him, and he with Me.

—Revelation 3:20 (NKJV)

This verse directly aligns with the imagery of the Savior persistently seeking the man's heart, and it beautifully illustrates the transformative power of opening oneself to salvation. It emphasizes the personal relationship with the Savior and the peace and purpose that come from living in alignment with His will.

Chapter

8

The Sinful Soldier

The boy, now the Sinful Soldier, had undergone a profound transformation. He no longer feared the darkness but faced it with the strength of his faith. His journey was not about avoiding sin but about understanding it, confronting it, and overcoming it through the grace of *the Savior*. The Sinful Solider and the Beautiful Queen, now united in their faith, walked together in harmony, their love a testament to the power of redemption.

The Sinful Soldier had become whole again, not through his own efforts, but through the mercy and wisdom of *the Savior*. And in that *peace*, he knew that no matter what lay ahead, he was no longer lost. He had found his purpose, and with it, the freedom to live a life of true success—a success not measured by the world's standards, but by the strength of his soul.

And He said to me, "My grace is sufficient for you, for My strength is made perfect in weakness." Therefore most gladly I will rather boast in my infirmities, that the power of Christ may rest upon me.

—II Corinthians 12:9 (NKJV)

This verse beautifully captures the Sinful Soldier's realization that his transformation and victory over sin are not through his own strength but through the grace of the Savior. It emphasizes the power of redemption, the strength found in faith, and how true success comes from embracing God's grace, not worldly accomplishments.

Epilogue

The Gift of Life

We *know* the *past* because it happened. We *cherish* the *present* because it is a *gift*, and we have faith in the future, for it is unknown.

Conclusion

A New Dawn

In the grand tapestry of existence, we are all both the innocent child and the sinful soldier, navigating the trials of life with imperfect hearts. The boy's journey reminds us that no matter how far we stray, the Creator's grace is infinite, always calling us back to our truest selves.

His story is not just one of redemption but of transformation—a reminder that even in our darkest moments, there is light to be found. Each stumble, each failure, and every battle within shapes us into something greater, drawing us closer to the divine purpose we are meant to fulfill.

Life is a journey, not toward perfection but toward *peace*—toward the wholeness that comes from embracing our imperfections and seeking strength beyond ourselves. And as the boy stepped into his new dawn, so too can we. With every ending comes a beginning, and with every struggle the hope of victory.

The Creator's hand is always there, guiding, lifting, and loving us, even when we cannot see it. It is up to us to answer the call—to embrace the gift of life, the beauty of transformation, and the promise of a new dawn.